IT'S ALL IN THE NAME

Check out these other L'il D books!

**Coming soon:
#2 Take the Court**

Hey L'il D!
IT'S ALL IN THE NAME

By Bob Lanier
and Heather Goodyear

Illustrated by
Desire Grover

A
LITTLE APPLE
PAPERBACK

SCHOLASTIC INC.
New York   Toronto   London   Auckland   Sydney
Mexico City   New Delhi   Hong Kong   Buenos Aires

I'd like to dedicate this book to my wonderful mom and dad and my precious big sister, Geraldine. Their love, support, and guidance have been a constant source of inspiration and direction during my life's journey. My love to them always.
— B.L.

For Chris — thank you.
— H.G.

ISBN 0-439-40899-7
Text copyright © 2003 by Bob Lanier
Illustrations copyright © 2003 by Scholastic Inc.
All rights reserved. Published by Scholastic Inc.
SCHOLASTIC, LITTLE APPLE, and
associated logos are trademarks and/or registered
trademarks of Scholastic Inc.

12 11 10 9 8 7 6 5 4 3 2 1   3 4 5 6 7 8/0

Printed in the U.S.A.
First printing, February 2003

Dear Reader,

Thank you for picking up this book. It's all about when I was a kid — when people called me L'il Dobber, instead of Big Bob. Back before I played in the NBA.

I grew up in Buffalo, New York. I loved basketball and played every chance I got. Luckily, I had great friends to hang out with both on and off the court. We had a lot of fun adventures — and they're all included in these books.

Soon you'll meet me as a kid (remember, they call me L'il Dobber!). You'll also meet my friends Joe, Sam, and Gan. We are always up to something! We may not do the right thing all the time, but whatever we do, we learn from it. And we have a lot of fun!

And that's something I hope you do with this HEY L'IL D! book — have fun. Because believe me, reading is one of the most fun, most important things that you can do.

I hope you like my story.

Bob Lanier

IT'S ALL IN THE NAME

Contents

Chapter 1
Waiting

L'il Dobber was sitting with his back slouched against the wall in the narrow hall outside the bathroom door. The first day of the new school year and he was stuck waiting. Geraldine, his sister, was in the bathroom. L'il Dobber knocked on the door but got no answer.

I'll probably do a lot of waiting today, he thought. First, he would get into his new class and wait for the teacher to call out the name of every student. She would, of course, say his real name, Bob Lanier, and not his nickname, L'il Dobber. Then he would wait while his teacher went over all of the classroom and school rules.

L'il Dobber could hear his mom across the house getting pans out in the kitchen.

He reached his arm around again and knocked on the bathroom door, calling out his sister's nickname loudly.

"Jerdine, come on," he urged his sister. "Hurry up!"

"What?" Geraldine's voice came from behind the door.

"I told you what five minutes ago — hurry up," said L'il Dobber.

"I had to wait, too, you know, for Mom and Dit," Geraldine answered. "Dit" was their nickname for their dad.

"Dit was out of here an hour ago and you weren't waiting because you weren't even up yet."

Geraldine cracked the bathroom door enough to stick out her ebony face and stare down at L'il Dobber.

"Look, you better stop bugging me; you're not the only one that starts school to-

day. It's my first day of middle school. So, unlike you, I have to look good." The crack in the door closed.

"Come on, Jerdine," L'il Dobber said to the once-again closed door. "Doesn't starting fourth grade count for something?"

"Um, not that much. But I'll be out in two minutes. *If* you stop talking to me."

L'il Dobber stood up and went back to his room. No reason to keep sitting on the floor for what would be another ten minutes at least. Besides, he wouldn't tell Geraldine he was up early anyway.

He had the little bit nervous, little bit disappointed, little bit excited first-day-of-school feelings in his stomach. He'd give Geraldine a break today. But he wasn't going to be shut out of the bathroom every morning.

The Laniers' three-bedroom brick house all of a sudden filled with the smell of pancakes. L'il Dobber's stomach started to growl. He wished Geraldine would hurry so he could at least brush his teeth and get to the kitchen to eat.

He flopped backward onto his bed and looked around his room. The plain white walls were decorated with basketball stuff that he had found, made, or been given as a gift. He had drawn basketball jerseys on paper and hung up the numbers of some of his favorite NBA players. *Someday,* he thought, *I'm going to be a famous basketball player and hang my own jersey on the wall.*

L'il Dobber heard the bathroom door click. He jumped up, took three running steps,

and slid behind Geraldine into the bathroom while she was still standing in the doorway. He closed the door quick so she couldn't change her mind.

In the kitchen ten minutes later, L'il Dobber's mom gave him a hug good morning.

"I have to leave for crossing-guard duty in fifteen minutes," she said. "Sit down so we can eat and talk before I go."

L'il Dobber's mom loved to cook — and she was good at it. Almost every occasion was a reason to cook, including the first morning of a new school year. *Pancakes, warm syrup, and fresh orange juice — so far, not a bad start to the first day of school,* L'il Dobber thought.

"Geri, do you have your class schedule?"

"Yes, Mom," Geraldine answered.

"And Bobby, you remember you're in Room 333 with Ms. Wilson, right?"

"Yes. Joe is, too," L'il Dobber answered between bites of pancakes.

He was glad that he was in the same class as Joe because the two friends hadn't seen much of each other in the last month. Joe and his twin sister, Sam, had gone to spend three weeks in Philadelphia with their dad. Then L'il Dobber had spent a week in Tennessee at his grandma's.

"Isn't that nice for you and Joe," Mrs. Lanier said. "Now you pay attention in class, though, and tell Ms. Wilson I said 'hello.' I didn't get to holler at her during church last week since we were in Tennessee."

"I will. But maybe it would be better if you didn't know my teacher so well, Mom."

"As long as you do well in class it shouldn't worry you whether your teacher and I are friends or not. Geri enjoyed having her and you will, too. Now I have to get to work," Mrs. Lanier said, grabbing her stop sign.

"Y'all put your dishes in the sink and get your lunches and backpacks. And don't forget to make sure the door is locked when you leave."

"We won't," L'il Dobber and Geraldine said at the same time.

"Geri, I'll see you this afternoon. Bobby, I'll see you at the crossing."

Mrs. Lanier patted her hair down and waved good-bye as she hurried out the door.

L'il Dobber watched his mom leave. He didn't know if he was more nervous than excited or more excited than nervous, but those first-day-of-school feelings were hitting his stomach hard again.

Chapter 2
Good-bye, Summer

L'il Dobber walked down the sidewalk, bouncing his basketball. Geraldine turned left on her way to middle school and he headed right to Public School 17. All around L'il Dobber was the hubbub of busy Buffalo, New York. But he walked slowly, waiting to see his buddy Joe coming over from Brunswick Avenue. They always walked to school together, and this year would be no different.

At the corner ahead, L'il Dobber saw the sun flash off Joe's and Sam's reddish blond heads as they appeared. Joe turned to look and held a hand up "hello" when he saw L'il

Dobber coming. Sam waved as she and a friend went on ahead to school.

"What's up?" asked L'il Dobber when he caught up to Joe.

"Hey L'il D," Joe greeted him. "You ready for school?"

"I guess. It's cool that we're in the same class."

"Yeah, so is a new kid named Gan. I met him while you were gone. He lives right down the street from you."

"Gan?" asked L'il Dobber. "You mean like 'gone,' as in 'he's gone'? What kind of a name is that?"

"He's Chinese," Joe said. "I told him about you. He said he'd play basketball with us at lunch. That's cool, right?"

"Yeah, he can play with us," L'il Dobber said, thumping the basketball with his fingertips.

"Cool. How was Tennessee?" Joe asked.

"Great. I went fishing with my uncle Houston. We caught some really big catfish."

"How many?" asked Joe.

"Me, only four or five. My uncle Houston caught a lot, though."

"Did you stay at your grandma's?"

"Yeah, at Big Mama's. I helped a lot in her garden. We picked vegetables and she used them to cook for us. It was so good. How was Philly?"

"Cool. My dad took us to see the Liberty Bell and Betsy Ross's house. All that stuff we learned about in school last year."

"How's your dad doing?" asked L'il Dobber.

"OK. He's got a little house now and we all played ball in the driveway."

"That's cool," L'il Dobber said.

"Yeah. Mom said she really missed us while we were gone, though," said Joe.

L'il Dobber and Joe talked and walked a few more blocks on the busy main drag of Northland Avenue. They passed houses of kids they knew, the neighborhood grocery store, and the Boys and Girls Clubs.

More and more kids walked along the sidewalk as they got closer to school. L'il

Dobber and Joe greeted and joked with class-mates they hadn't seen all summer. L'il Dobber took note that he was still a good half foot taller than all of them.

Suddenly, Joe nudged L'il Dobber in the ribs and made him bobble his basketball.

"Brooks is heading this way," said Joe, nodding across the street.

L'il Dobber knew what was coming. He looked up and saw Brooks walking with his three sidekicks in tow.

"Hey, Feet," said Brooks as he approached L'il Dobber.

"Whaaz up, Feet?" his sidekicks all repeated.

"Quit calling me Feet," said L'il Dobber. "That's old and tired, man."

"Whatever, Feet," Brooks said. "Man, I'd hate it if *I* had to lug those big sneakers around all the time!"

Brooks and his sidekicks laughed. Then they disappeared into the crowd because they were almost at the corner where Mrs. Lanier worked. Brooks talked big in front of other

kids, but he would never pick on L'il Dobber in front of his mom.

"He's lame," L'il Dobber said angrily to Joe. "Calling me that just because I have big feet. I don't call him Mouth just 'cause he has a big mouth."

"And his mouth is a lot more annoying than your feet," Joe added, sticking up for L'il Dobber.

The boys reached the last corner to cross before the school.

"Hey, Mom."

"Hi, Mrs. Lanier."

"Hi, Bobby," his mom said, turning from the group of kids she had been talking to about their summer vacations.

"Nice to see you, Joe. Did you and Sam have a nice visit with your dad?"

"Yeah. It was fun."

"Bobby sure wished you were here," Mrs. Lanier said, then looked at L'il Dobber.

"Did you and Geri have any trouble getting off to school?" his mom asked.

"None," he answered.

"Good. Time to cross."

Enough kids were waiting at the corner, so L'il Dobber's mom walked into the busy street when there was a break in traffic. She raised her stop sign.

"Have a good day," she told all the kids moving through the crosswalk.

"Enjoy your first day, son," she said to L'il Dobber and squeezed his shoulder as he passed.

"Yes, ma'am," said L'il Dobber as he crossed the street to the front of the school.

He walked toward the main doors and the first-day-of-school feeling in his stomach was replaced with a good-bye-to-summer feeling.

L'il Dobber liked school because he was curious and enjoyed learning. But he really lived for recess and the hours between the end of school and dinnertime. That was when he got to play basketball and be with his friends.

L'il Dobber looked over other kids' heads as he walked through the school doors. He was excited about school but he would miss playing hoops all day. So, he couldn't help walking a little slower as he and Joe started down the hall and went to find Room 333.

Chapter 3
Why "L'il Dobber"?

The fourth-grade classes at Public School 17 had made it through all of the first-morning back-to-school business and now had some time to themselves at lunch recess.

L'il Dobber, Joe, and Gan jogged to the basketball hoop in the cement school yard. L'il Dobber had met Gan in the lunchroom and they all ate lunch together. He thought right away they would be friends.

As they got to the court, Gan yelled, "Hey L'il D, where'd you get your name? Why do people call you L'il Dobber?"

"It's like this," L'il Dobber yelled back to

be heard over the noise of the other kids and the traffic along the street.

"My dad was a really great basketball player when he was a kid. He holds a bunch of records. Everyone who went to Bennett High School knows about him."

"Yeah, my dad does," said Joe.

"His Friday-night games were packed because his team was the best in Buffalo. He could really fill it up," L'il Dobber continued.

"My dad went to watch those games," Joe added in.

"Anyway, they all called him Big Dobber. My family started calling me L'il Dobber 'cause I want to be just like my dad. And the nickname stuck."

Gan tossed a shot toward the basket and said, "I should have a nickname, too. Every time I watch a basketball game on TV, all the stars have catchy nicknames. I'm just Gan. If I'm gonna be a star, I need a new name."

"*You're* gonna be a basketball star?" L'il Dobber grinned as he looked at Gan, who only came up to his shoulder.

"Yeah. I'll be a guard," Gan said, nodding, "and all the great guards have nicknames. You guys can think about it for a while and come up with a good one."

"Nice shot, L'il D," Joe called as he caught the ball falling through the hoop. Joe spun, dribbled once, shot the ball back up and through the hoop. Gan took it and dribbled to the free throw line to shoot.

"What can you call me?" he asked as he set up his shot. "It doesn't even have to do with basketball, I guess. I do other stuff, too."

"Well, we sure can't call you Ace," joked Joe. "You said you usually get C's on tests."

"Yeah, you gave three wrong answers during the math speed drill this morning," L'il Dobber joined in.

As Joe and L'il Dobber laughed, Joe teased, "We didn't know 12 times 2 was 42!"

"Even I know 12 times 2 is 24," chimed in Sam, Joe's twin sister, as she ran up to meet them.

"You didn't start without me, did you?" she questioned with her hands on her hips.

She hated that they left her out of things sometimes. They did let her play basketball with them, though. She could hold her own against them, up and down the court.

The fact that she played sports with the boys also made her one of their friends — even if she was Joe's sister.

"Sam, you remember Gan from last week, right?" asked Joe. Gan and Sam said "hey" as they nodded to each other.

"Let's divide up," said Joe, anxious to play. "L'il Dobber and Sam, and I'll play with Gan. You guys get the ball first."

In the school yard there was room for only one basket and a painted key. Because they played every day, it was understood that L'il Dobber and his friends got the hoop during recesses. Sometimes other kids joined them, but since it was such a small area it was usually just them on the court.

"Gan wants a nickname," L'il Dobber told Sam as she took the ball to the top of the key.

"Like my name's Samantha, but I get called Sam?"

"No," Gan answered. "I want a nickname that tells something I do."

"What about Double Dribble? I saw you shooting as I ran over here and you seem to do that well," Sam said teasingly.

"Very funny," Gan said. "No. I want to be Clutch or something catchy like that."

"Enough talking and dribbling," cut in Joe. "Let's play."

Joe lunged at Sam. She cut left and dribbled past.

They got down to the business of playing basketball with what time they had left. Gan was still daydreaming about nicknames, and he missed three passes and four shots. Joe was on today, though, and without much help from Gan they still beat L'il Dobber and Sam by four points.

The recess whistle blew as the last of Joe's shots went up and in, despite a block from Sam. L'il Dobber grabbed the basketball and they joined the rush of kids crowding toward the propped-open metal door and an afternoon of classes.

Chapter 4
Dinner Talk

At home that night, L'il Dobber and his family were sitting in the kitchen having dinner and listening to Geraldine talk about her first day of sixth grade. L'il Dobber was into his third helping of greens and ham hocks when his turn finally came to tell everyone about *his* first day at school.

"I met a new kid in class today named Gan. He moved in five houses down where the Dixons lived."

"I'll have to stop in and welcome them tomorrow," said Mrs. Lanier.

"He played ball with us at lunch today. I

think he could be good if he'd wake up a little on the court."

"How'd you play today? Did you represent?" his dad asked.

"I made eight out of eleven hoops, Dit, and we almost beat them."

"Well, this is where it starts, L'il Dobber. If you want to be a great player, just keep practicing and playing with your friends."

"I do want to be a great player — just like you."

"I'm glad recess was a good part of your day," L'il Dobber's mom said. "But what did you get done in class?"

"Just first-day stuff," L'il Dobber answered. "Filled out info cards, got our books, played a game to learn everyone's names. Oh, and we did some math drills, too. But no homework until next week, Ms. Wilson said."

"I remember those easy days," Geraldine said, trying to sound very wise and grown up.

"I already have homework tonight since I'm not in the *lower* grades anymore," she added.

"Your grades can't get any *lower*," L'il Dobber said back.

"I know you will both try hard in school this year," L'il Dobber's mom said before either of them could make another comment. "Do your best and your grades will be your best, too."

"I think we're all done here," his mom continued, looking around at the empty dishes on the table. "With no homework tonight, Bobby, you can help me clear the table and tell me more about your day."

Later in the week, L'il Dobber was invited to Gan's house for dinner. He and Gan were sitting and talking to Gan's mother as she chopped vegetables for dinner.

Gan had learned the best time to get attention was to hang around his mom while she was doing work and not to wait until she had time to sit down. That was when all his older brothers and sisters pounced on her to ask their questions.

"I need a nickname like L'il Dobber has,"

Gan said matter-of-factly. "His dad was called Big Dobber because he was a great high school basketball player."

"I was actually wondering where your name came from," Mrs. Xu said to L'il Dobber.

"Why do you always just call me Gan, Mom?" Gan asked.

"Because that's your name," Mrs. Xu answered, dumping the chopped vegetables into the skillet.

"I know. I just think it would be more special to call me Slam or Lucky like a sports star," Gan said, "or Row, like we call Uncle Jie."

Mrs. Xu laughed. "Uncle Jie got that nickname from many summers of family canoe trips when we were growing up. None of us ever wanted to be in a canoe with Jie because he would get us in the worst situations. We'd spin around and around in the current or head right back toward the shore."

"It sounds like fun," said L'il Dobber.

"Yes, and it would be funny later," said Mrs. Xu. "But in the middle of the river we would yell at him, 'Row! Row!' while we battled against the waters. We yelled 'row' at him so much that we started calling him Row all the time. Sometimes a nickname comes out of a funny time in life and it just sticks."

"I do funny things," Gan pointed out.

"You do," she said and handed him eight plates and L'il Dobber eight napkins, "but nothing has stuck, yet. Please put these on the table."

"You know," Mrs. Xu continued when Gan and L'il Dobber returned from the dining room, "we named you Gan because it means courageous. Courage is an important characteristic. To have people think of you as brave would be better than having them think of a nickname for you."

Mrs. Xu stirred the rice in the steamer, checked once more on the chicken, and opened a drawer to count out silverware. She gave the utensils to Gan and L'il Dobber, and they headed back to the dining room to set each place.

"I do like my name," Gan told his mother

as she came in with the glasses. "I think I'll keep working on getting a nickname, though."

"Well, even if you get a nickname, it's what you do and how you treat others that is most important," Mrs. Xu said. As she went to get the food from the kitchen, she called over her shoulder, "Would you two please tell everyone it is time for dinner?"

A few minutes later, the dining room was filled with voices. Seven people, plus L'il Dobber tonight, were all talking at once. Gan wanted to ask his brothers and sisters for some nickname ideas. He didn't get the chance, though, because Gan's oldest brother, Hong, was going to take a test tomorrow to get his driver's license.

Gan's parents were quizzing Hong over sign meanings and speed limits.

"I'm glad I don't need to know all of this for another six years," Gan said with a sigh of relief. "I know to stop at a red light and go on a green light. That's enough for me right now."

The rest of the Xu family and L'il Dobber continued talking and eating, but Gan's thoughts drifted back to ideas for a nickname.

L'il Dobber, however, was enjoying what he learned in the conversation. He thought it would be fun to show off his new knowledge the next time his family drove somewhere in the car — especially to Geraldine.

Chapter 5
Speaking Up in Class

A few weeks later, L'il Dobber was sitting at his desk, paying attention to the front of the classroom. He couldn't wait to learn about explorers in social studies. He had spent the last week memorizing places on the globe. Learning about explorers sounded a lot more exciting.

He listened as Ms. Wilson explained, "We learned about the continents and oceans last week, and now we will begin talking about some of the brave people who sailed across the oceans and walked across the continents to discover what became the United States. To start, can anyone name any explorers?"

Hands shot up all over the class.

"Yes, Jacqui?" Ms. Wilson asked.

"Christopher Columbus."

The hands in the class went down.

"Yes, Christopher Columbus was an explorer," Ms. Wilson answered. "He sailed from Spain and we will learn about him. Are there other explorers that anyone can name?"

She paused and waited for hands. L'il Dobber looked around the room to see if other kids knew any. He had known Christopher Columbus, but that was it.

"No others?" Ms. Wilson asked. "Whew, we have a lot to learn, then."

"We are going to do a project," she said, facing the class. "Look up here at this bulletin board."

L'il Dobber looked and saw a light blue background with the shapes of the continents on it — just like on a map of the world.

The title "Footprints to the United States" ran across the top.

"As a class, we will be finishing this board," Ms. Wilson said. "I will put you in pairs and each pair will receive a piece of dark blue paper, an index card, and the name of an explorer."

Ms. Wilson held up the paper.

L'il Dobber listened as she explained that each pair was supposed to use the blue paper to trace one of their footprints, cut it out, and write their explorer's name on it. Then they would use the index card to write a paragraph about the explorer. When they finished, they were supposed to staple the footprint and the card up on the bulletin board.

"Are there any questions before I pair you up?" Ms. Wilson asked.

Brooks's hand shot up.

"Yes, Brooks?"

L'il Dobber was surprised when he heard Brooks ask, "Should L'il Dobber trace his foot?"

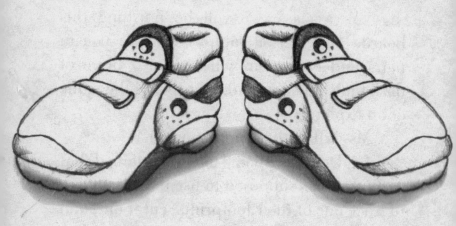

"Excuse me?" Ms. Wilson said.

"Well, if he does, won't it cover the whole bulletin board and not leave any room for the rest of us?" Brooks asked.

A few kids giggled. Then the whole class was laughing.

L'il Dobber stared down at his desk and tried to sit very still. He thought that maybe if he didn't look at anyone they wouldn't look at him.

L'il Dobber heard Ms. Wilson respond, "Brooks, since you need to waste my class time, I will waste *your* recess time. While the rest of the class enjoys a short break this afternoon, you will spend some time in here chatting with me about respect and appropriate classroom behavior."

"Yes, ma'am," Brooks answered quietly.

L'il Dobber noticed out of the corner of his eye that Ms. Wilson was nice enough to not look at him the whole time she was scolding Brooks. He would've felt even worse if she had looked at him and made the other kids think he needed her to stick up for him.

That afternoon at recess, L'il Dobber, Gan, Joe, and Sam were tossing the basketball around as usual. Gan was asking again about a nickname when L'il Dobber saw Brooks heading out the school door.

When Brooks got to where they were playing, L'il Dobber paused with the basketball in his hand and asked him sarcastically, "Fun recess so far?"

Brooks just kept his head down, mumbled a "shut up," and walked past.

L'il Dobber was glad that Brooks wasn't jawing at him for once. He wondered how long it would last.

Chapter 6
See Ya, Brooks!

L'il Dobber stewed about Brooks picking on him, and by the next evening he was upset enough to tell his mom about it. She was scrubbing pots at the sink after dinner and he and Geraldine were doing homework at the kitchen table.

"Do you think I got the wrong feet?" L'il Dobber asked his mom.

"Those are the feet you were given the day you were born, so I'm sure they're a perfect fit," his mom answered.

"Maybe I've got some kind of mutant gene."

Mrs. Lanier gave L'il Dobber a sideways look with a raised eyebrow.

"What if they keep growing and growing and never stop?" he asked.

"I'm pretty sure that won't happen. In fact, I'm certain."

"But they're so big already," L'il Dobber complained. "The next closest shoe size in my class is two whole sizes smaller than me."

"And each of those children has something about themselves they don't like, just as you don't like your feet," his mom said.

L'il Dobber sat quiet for a moment.

"Brooks and his three buddies always call me Feet. It's embarrassing."

"I know," his mom said and stopped scrubbing the pots to look at him. "Ms. Wilson told me as I was leaving school after duty yesterday."

"I hate it when they call me Feet," L'il Dobber said as his dad walked into the kitchen.

"Well, you do have big feet," Geraldine said, as if he didn't know that.

"That's not really helpful right now, Geri," Mrs. Lanier said.

"I didn't mean they should tease him. If I ever hear them, they'll have to deal with me. I'm just saying L'il Dobber's feet *are* big."

"You've said enough," Mrs. Lanier told her. "Let your dad and me talk to Bobby, please."

Geraldine went back to her homework. L'il Dobber's mom turned to him and said,

"Maybe they call you Feet because they know it bugs you."

"I don't see how it wouldn't."

L'il Dobber's dad looked at him and said, "Listen, L'il Dobber. You don't let those kids run you home. You gotta learn how to be strong and they'll back down."

"Kids can be mean sometimes, Bobby, but you know you're special," his mom said reassuringly. "Don't let them make you think otherwise. Just try to ignore them."

L'il Dobber shrugged. His mom gave him a sympathetic look and said, "Don't mind your feet or what other kids say. Those feet will take you to great places.

"Now finish up that reading and you can watch some sports with Dit before bed."

L'il Dobber found out the next day at lunch recess that Brooks's quietness didn't last long. L'il Dobber spun with a dribble and saw Brooks and his friends standing at the top of the key.

"Hey, Feet, you may be getting some visitors soon," Brooks shouted.

"Huh?" L'il Dobber looked puzzled as he picked up his dribble and faced Brooks.

"I watched a Discovery Channel show on Big Foot last night. They're looking for you way out in the woods of Oregon. I called in and set them straight. So, don't be surprised if they come knocking on your door."

Joe, Sam, and Gan stood behind L'il Dobber and gave Brooks and his friends nasty looks.

Okay, thought L'il Dobber. *I'm not letting them bother me this time.*

Without a word to Brooks, he turned and tossed the ball to Gan. "Forget him," he said to his friends. "Let's play."

Gan, Joe, and Sam shrugged and started tossing the ball around again.

Brooks and his friends stared for a minute. Then they strolled to the other end of the school yard.

"See ya," mumbled L'il Dobber, as he watched them walk away.

"That was great!" Joe exclaimed.

"Maybe my mom and dad were right," L'il Dobber said. "They told me to just ignore him."

"It sure worked this time," Sam said.

"Now we can get back to our game," said L'il Dobber.

"How about Express for my nickname?" Gan asked and dribbled as fast as he could toward the basket for a layup.

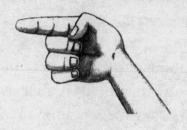

Chapter 7
Farsight

The next Monday, L'il Dobber and Gan were in line on the way into class.

"Hey, I thought of some nicknames for you last night," L'il Dobber said.

"That's great!" exclaimed Gan excitedly. "Tell me."

"You've got a pretty thick pair of glasses," L'il Dobber explained as they inched forward into the classroom. "How about Four Eyes, Pop Bottles, or Farsight?"

Gan was about to say a definite no when he heard: "I get it. Farsight. That's a good one," laughed Tyler, the kid behind them who overheard.

Gan had a feeling it was bad that, of all the boys, Tyler had heard. Gan had already learned that Tyler couldn't keep anything he found funny to himself.

Gan sighed as Tyler immediately turned to the kids behind him and said, "Gan wants to be called Farsight from now on. It's his new nickname."

During the week, the other kids began to call Gan Farsight. When he tripped in gym class — Farsight. When he read the wrong paragraph during social studies — Farsight. When he didn't see L'il Dobber and Joe already sitting at a table, L'il Dobber yelled across the lunchroom, "Farsight — over here, man."

The nickname was catching on and Gan didn't like it. Kids always made fun of other kids with glasses. He didn't want a nickname based on his glasses. *This isn't a nickname,* thought Gan. *This is just a joke to them — a joke on me.*

He was quiet on the walk home from school Friday, as L'il Dobber and Joe talked about meeting at the park after they checked in at home.

"I can play. I just have to call my mom at work," said Joe.

"What about Sam?" asked L'il Dobber.

"I'll ask her. Gan, you playing today?"

"I don't know."

"You got something going on?" asked L'il Dobber.

"No. I'll be there, I guess," Gan answered.

"Something wrong?" Joe asked as they got to the corner of Brunswick and Northland Avenue where Joe turned to go home.

"No, I'll see you at the park," said Gan and then left them standing at the corner as he walked ahead to his house.

*   *   *

A half hour later, L'il Dobber, Joe, Gan, and Sam met at Delaware Park. They played ball there any day they could. The four of them walked through the gate in the fence and across the grass to the cement-slab court.

The baskets were tall and rusty and the paint lines were faint. But it was a full court and the chain nets made a nice *ka-ching* sound when a hoop was made.

Today, they didn't divide up into teams. They played fast breaks. Three of them would streak to the other end of the court, and the fourth would try to hit them with a long pass.

Gan had a good arm so he was on target with his passes. Being the tallest, L'il Dobber reached up and caught the most to shoot.

They had played for twenty minutes when Gan threw a bad pass to the other end of the court. The ball veered to the far left and bounced out of bounds. It was the first and only bad pass he had made all day.

Sam yelled from the other end of the court, "Hey, Farsight, we're right here. Where are you throwing?"

They all came trotting back to where Gan stood, and L'il Dobber flipped the ball to him, "Try again, Farsight," he said with a smile, and they took off running.

Gan threw the ball as hard as he could and it slammed the backboard at the other end. He spun and started off the court.

"What was that?" called Joe.

"Get real!" Gan spun back around. "Farsight is not a nickname. You guys are just cutting me down."

He ran to the gate and left the park.

L'il Dobber, Joe, and Sam stared after him.

"Wow, what just happened?" Joe asked in amazement.

"What happened is that we made him mad," L'il Dobber said.

"We were just joking," said Sam.

"I guess he didn't think it was as funny as we all did," L'il Dobber said.

"I feel bad that we hurt his feelings," said Sam.

"I feel bad I was the one who thought of Farsight in the first place," L'il Dobber said. "I didn't think it sounded mean, but Gan did."

"He's being too sensitive," Joe said.

"Maybe," said L'il Dobber, sounding unsure.

"Everyone has something about themselves they don't like," Joe pointed out.

"Am I too touchy when I get mad at Brooks calling me Feet?" L'il Dobber asked him.

"No."

"Well, it's the same thing, I guess. I don't like my feet and maybe Gan doesn't like his glasses," L'il Dobber said thoughtfully.

"So we shouldn't call him a nickname about them," said Sam.

"Good point," said Joe.

"But how do we apologize?" asked Sam.

"First, we should stop calling him Farsight," L'il Dobber said.

"Definitely," the other two agreed.

"Let's think of a better nickname for him," Joe suggested.

"We could come up with some and let him choose this time," Sam said.

"That might make him feel better," L'il Dobber said as he jogged after the basketball, which had bounced away after Gan's throw.

L'il Dobber returned to the court and sat down on the ball. Joe and Sam sat on either side of him and they kicked around ideas for a couple of minutes. They thought of two nicknames that Gan might like.

"Let's go tell him now," Sam said and jumped up.

"No," Joe said. "We have to get home before Mom does, to help with dinner. We better go."

"Let's tell him as soon as we see him tomorrow," L'il Dobber said as they walked toward the park gate.

"He'll be mad at us all night, though," Sam said sadly.

"That's OK. We'll make up for it when he hears our great ideas for nicknames," Joe said.

"He'll definitely like these," said L'il Dobber, and he threw his basketball up over the fence and then caught it on the other side as he exited through the gate.

Chapter 8
New Ideas

The lunchtime basketball game was put on hold the next day. L'il Dobber, Joe, and Sam were standing by the school yard basket watching for Gan. He hadn't walked to school or eaten lunch with them.

Gan finally came out to the playground and looked around, trying to decide where to go if he wasn't going to play basketball.

"Gan, over here," L'il Dobber yelled.

Gan looked over, and, even though he was mad, he was grateful he didn't have to try and ignore them anymore. He didn't know too many other kids yet and, besides, L'il Dobber,

Joe, and Sam had become his best friends. He walked over to the basket.

"We were waiting for you," Sam said when he came up to them.

"Sorry we called you Farsight so much," Joe said, starting their apology.

"We thought you didn't care, but we should've asked you," L'il Dobber said.

"Sorry it wasn't the kind of nickname you wanted," Sam said.

"Thanks, you guys," Gan replied and sounded relieved. "Maybe if you stop calling me that, everyone else will, too."

"Since you really did want a nickname," Sam began, "we thought of some for you. We'll let you pick this time."

"Mine first," Joe spoke up. "How about Bull's-eye? Your passes are usually straight and on target like an arrow. Get it? Bull's-eye would be a great nickname."

Gan laughed. "That's not bad."

Joe smiled and looked proud.

"That's a cool one," L'il Dobber agreed. "But I thought we could call you G. Just the

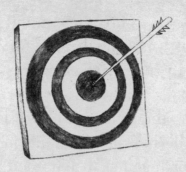

first letter of your name. It makes you sound cool. Like —'Hey, G.' or 'Way to go, G!'"

"Those were the best ones we thought of," Sam said. "What do you think?"

"I like them both. But you don't have to call me either of them," Gan said.

"I thought about it," Gan continued. "And I figure sometime the right nickname will come along like it did for my uncle or you, L'il Dobber. I'll just wait."

L'il Dobber, Joe, and Sam all nodded.

"Cool," Joe said.

"Gan, you pick teams for what time we have left," L'il Dobber said.

"OK. Me and you, Joe and Sam. Joe, you take the ball first."

There were only a few minutes left of recess, but it was enough time for L'il Dobber and Gan to score sixteen points to Joe and Sam's ten.

When the whistle blew, L'il Dobber grabbed the ball and they all jogged to the school door together. It felt good not to have anyone mad anymore.

Chapter 9
Good Eyes, Great Courage

It was the beginning of lunch recess a week later, and L'il Dobber's class was rushing out into the school yard. "That taxi's gonna hit that car," Gan blurted out.

Screech! Bam!

Metal and glass smashed just as Gan finished shouting.

All the kids ran to the fence and stared in awe at the two cars with crumpled front ends. It was quite the show for recess!

The taxi driver jumped out of his empty cab and ran to the old man who was pushing open the door and trying to swing his legs out

of his car. The taxi driver looked mad, and the old man looked dazed.

"You hit me," yelled the taxi driver accusingly. "You drove through a red light. You hit me!"

The old man said nothing, just stared. He seemed to take a long time getting out of the car.

A siren whined in the distance and got closer. The crowd of kids turned their heads as the police car zigged and zagged down the street through the cars that were jamming up.

One police officer jumped out and started directing traffic. The other police officer ran over to the banged-up cars and led the taxi driver to the sidewalk, right in front of the fence where the children stood.

"He hit me!" The taxi driver was talking very fast and loud. "He drove through a red light right in front of me and hit me. I'm a good driver. He hit *me*."

The police officer listened and took notes. "Did anyone say they saw the accident?"

"No."

"No one else in any car?"

"No."

"Well, I'll ask around. Are you hurt?"

"No. But my car is."

"May I see your license?"

The officer looked at the taxi driver's license and then said, "Thank you, Mr. Lewis. Please stay right here, sir." He walked across the street to the old man, who was shaking his head while his car was being attached to a tow truck.

As the police officer walked away, Gan whispered to L'il Dobber, "He's lying. I saw it happen, and the taxi driver drove when the light was red." Gan was remembering his family's dinner conversation the night before Hong took his driving test. The taxi driver had a red light, so he should have been stopped.

"You sure?" L'il Dobber questioned him.

"Yes, and look. No one else will tell the police officers they saw it."

They looked and saw other drivers shaking their heads at the officer.

"You should tell Ms. Grant," L'il Dobber said.

Gan turned into the crowd and worked his way to the recess attendant. She listened to Gan and then put her hand on his shoulder and walked him back to the fence by the taxi driver. The police officer returned.

"At this time, no tickets can be issued, due to no witnesses and the conflicting story of the other driver," began the officer.

"Excuse me, officer," said Ms. Grant. "I have a boy here who saw the accident."

The officer looked through the fence at Gan with a curious expression.

"Did you see it clearly?"

"Yes. I knew the taxi was going to hit the car," Gan said, feeling many eyes looking at him. He tried to focus on the police officer.

"Can you tell me how you knew that?"

"When I was walking from the school door to the basketball hoop, I was looking hard at the stopped traffic. When the cars on the side street started to drive, I saw the taxi

move, too. I looked up and saw the taxi had a red light. It happened so fast, but when I saw him move, I knew he was going to hit the other car."

While Gan had been talking, the crowd of kids had been led in from recess. The school yard was empty and quiet, completely different from the noise Gan was used to. Only the principal, Mrs. Briers, who had come outside, and Ms. Grant now stood by him.

"This kid doesn't know," complained the taxi driver.

"I do know," Gan said confidently to the police officer.

"This man knows, too," said the other officer to her partner as she stepped up from the street with another man next to her.

"He approached me after the traffic cleared and said he witnessed the accident from behind the car that was hit. The taxi went through a red light."

She looked at the taxi driver and finished, "He gave a statement and is willing to testify if needed."

The taxi driver looked at the officers, Gan, and the other witness. His expression of anger turned to pleading.

"I can't get a ticket. My boss will be very angry. *Please*, I *cannot* get a ticket."

"Looks like you're at fault, Mr. Lewis," said the first officer. "Did you go through the red light?"

"I guess," said the taxi driver quietly.

"Come with me please, sir."

The second officer led the taxi driver over to the police car and pulled out a ticket book. The first police officer turned his attention again to Gan.

"I'm Officer Weston. What is your name?"

"I'm Gan Xu."

"You have good eyes, Gan. I'm glad you were paying attention. You were very courageous to speak up and tell the truth."

"Thank you," Gan replied to the officer's compliments.

"I'll need to write down your address and telephone number, please, and then you can get back to school."

Gan gave the police officer the information and then walked across the school yard with Ms. Grant and Mrs. Briers. They both told Gan how proud they were of him for having the courage to tell the truth.

Chapter 10
Shining with Fame

L'il Dobber, Joe, Sam, and the rest of the fourth graders couldn't wait to hear Gan's story after school. He was, of course, the sensation of the day.

Gan told his story excitedly as they walked into the school yard. A group of kids surrounded him, quietly shuffling through the recently fallen leaves, trying to hear every word. After Gan finished, everyone started talking at once.

"You were so brave!"

"That took a lot of courage."

"He just did what was right."

"The cops should give you a medal."

"Did the cops use their guns?"

"Of course not. They didn't need their guns!"

"Hey, we really should call you Farsight now," said L'il Dobber. "You saw the accident when no one else did."

"That's right," agreed a boy in the group.

"Good job, Farsight," said someone else.

"Good eyes, Farsight," chimed in another.

After being called that name a week ago and hating it, Gan thought now it had a new ring. It didn't sound mean anymore, it sounded respectful. Gan realized a good nickname should make the person feel special.

As the kids began to head separate ways to their homes Gan heard many of them say, "Bye, Farsight" or "See ya', Farsight."

"That's cool, you guys," Gan said to them. "You can call me Farsight now if you want — I like it. But I really want to be called Gan. I like that best."

Gan moved on toward home with L'il

Dobber, Joe, and Sam. He felt good about himself *and* about his real name.

L'il Dobber was standing next to his front porch that night, tossing his basketball against the front steps. A couple of leaves from the big maple in the yard brushed against the back of his legs, and, as he turned to look, he saw a police car driving past his house. He watched the car as it stopped in front of the Xu house.

L'il Dobber caught and held the ball and watched with interest as a police officer went up to Gan's house. When the door opened, L'il Dobber watched him shake hands with Gan and then Gan's parents.

Mrs. Lanier came out the front door to call L'il Dobber for dinner. She turned toward where he was looking.

"What is happening at Gan's house?" she asked worriedly, as she walked down the steps to stand next to him.

"I don't think anything bad," L'il Dobber

said, so she wouldn't get upset. "I'm pretty sure the officer at his house is the one Gan talked to about the car accident he saw at lunch today. Maybe he came to tell Gan's parents how Gan told the truth and helped them figure out what happened."

L'il Dobber told his mom all about how Gan had told the police officer the truth about what he had seen.

"That was very brave," L'il Dobber's mom said admiringly.

"Gan said that's what his name means. Courageous. Brave."

"Well, he certainly behaved that way today."

"What does Bob mean?" L'il Dobber asked.

"Bob actually means, 'shining with fame,'" his mom said.

"Wow. That'll be perfect when I'm a famous basketball player," L'il Dobber said excitedly.

"That's true." His mom laughed. "Between

being nicknamed L'il Dobber after your dad and being named Bob, you have two very special names to live up to."

She turned back toward the house and motioned for L'il Dobber to follow.

Smiling at him, L'il Dobber's mom said, "Now let's go eat dinner so you can grow up healthy and shine with fame."

Tell us about your next adventure!

TAKE THE COURT

L'il Dobber walked out the metal door to lunch recess two days later and stopped so quickly that Joe and Gan ran right into his back.

"What's going on?" L'il Dobber yelled in shock.

Brooks and his sidekicks were grouped under the basket, shooting hoops.

L'il Dobber, Joe, and Gan ran over to the small court.

"What are you guys doing?" demanded L'il Dobber.

"Playing a little hoops, Feet," Brooks said, as if they did it everyday.

"Obviously," said Brooks's pals together.

"We play here at recess," L'il Dobber told them.

"Not today," said Brooks. He caught the next pass and held the ball at his side.

"Yeah," the sidekicks agreed.

"And not until we want to give the court up," said Brooks.

"Yeah," the pals said again.

"I hear hopscotch is open," Brooks said to L'il Dobber. "You could draw the squares bigger so your feet will fit inside."

Sam ran up just as Brooks and his buddies started tossing the basketball again.

"What's going on here?" Sam demanded.

Brooks dribbled the ball in place and stared at Sam.

"Feet can clue you in," he said to her.

"Don't call L'il Dobber, 'Feet,'" Sam said

angrily. Then she turned to L'il Dobber. "What's going on?"

"Brooks and his pals think they're going to take over the court at recess," said L'il Dobber.

"Why?" Sam asked Brooks. "You don't like basketball as much as we do."

"No, but I like taking the court from you four," said Brooks.

Ms. Grant, the recess attendant, came over to the two groups glaring at each other on the court.

"Do I need to settle something between all of you today?" she asked.

Brooks looked at L'il Dobber, challenging him to get Ms. Grant to help them.

"No, we're all set," L'il Dobber said. It was like a playground code — they would try to fix the problem by themselves before getting a teacher involved.

"Let's go, guys," L'il Dobber said miserably.

L'il Dobber turned and dribbled his basketball over to the far fence. Joe, Sam, and

Gan followed. They all sat down and leaned their backs against the jangling metal. Waiting out the rest of lunch recess, they stared at what they had always believed was *their* court.

About the Authors

Bob Lanier is a basketball legend and a member of the Basketball Hall of Fame. A graduate of St. Bonaventure University, he has been hailed as much for his work in the community as for his play on the court. Winner of numerous awards and honors, he currently serves as Special Assistant to NBA Commissioner David Stern and as Captain of the NBA's All-Star Reading Team.

Like L'il Dobber, Bob has faced life's challenges head-on with a positive attitude and a never-ending belief in the power and value of reading and education.

Bob and his wife, Rose, have eight children and reside in Scottsdale, Arizona.

Heather Goodyear started creative writing in the first grade, with poems she wrote on scraps of paper. Her teacher gave her a blank notebook and said, "Be sure to let me know when you publish your first book." Hey L'il D! is her first series.

Sports were an important part of Heather's childhood in Michigan. As the only girl in a close family with two brothers, she learned early to hold her own in living room wrestling matches, driveway basketball contests, and family football games.

Heather says that this love of sports, and her classroom experience as a teacher, makes Hey L'il D! especially fun for her to write.

Heather lives in Arizona with her husband, Chris, and their three young children.